Bruno
the Bear

by
W.G. Van de Hulst

illustrated by
Willem G. Van de Hulst, Jr.

INHERITANCE PUBLICATIONS
NEERLANDIA, ALBERTA, CANADA
PELLA, IOWA, U.S.A.

Library and Archives Canada Cataloguing in Publication
Hulst, W. G. van de (Willem Gerrit), 1879-1963
[Bruun de beer. English]
        Bruno the bear / by W.G. Van de Hulst ; illustrated by Willem
G. Van de Hulst, Jr. ; [translated by Harry der Nederlanden and
Theodore   Plantinga].
(Stories children love ; 3)
Translation of: Bruun de beer.
Originally published: St. Catharines, Ontario : Paideia Press, 1978.
ISBN 978-1-928136-03-3 (pbk.)
        I. Hulst, Willem G. van de (Willem Gerrit), 1917-, illustrator
II. Nederlanden, Harry der translator   III. Plantinga, Theodore, 1947-,
translator IV. Title. V. Title: Bruun de beer. English VI. Series: Hulst,
W. G. van de (Willem Gerrit), 1879-1963 Stories children love ; 3
PZ7.H873985Bru 2014   j839.313'62   C2014-903595-0

Library of Congress Cataloging-in-Publication Data
Hulst, W. G. van de (Willem Gerrit), 1879-1963.
[Bruun de beer. English.]
Bruno the bear / by W.G. Van de Hulst ; illustrated by Willem G. Van de Hulst, Jr. ; edited
by Paulina Janssen.
pages cm. — (Stories children love ; #3)
"Originally published in Dutch as Bruun de beer. Original translations done by Harry der
Nederlanden and Theodore Plantinga for Paideia Press, St. Catharines-Ontario-Canada."
Summary: Jimmy and Joe, unaware that their little sister Rosie is sick, tie a string to her
teddy bear and dangle it over the creek, but when the string breaks the rowdy boys try to
rescue Bruno before Rosie or their parents find out what they did.
ISBN 978-1-928136-03-3
[1. Teddy bears—Fiction. 2. Toys—Fiction. 3. Brothers and sisters—Fiction. 4.
Behavior—Fiction. 5. Lost and found possessions—Fiction. 6. Sick—Fiction.] I. Hulst,
Willem G. van de (Willem Gerrit), 1917- illustrator. II. Title.
PZ7.H887Bru 2014   [E]—dc23   2014017983

Originally published in Dutch as *Bruun de beer*
Cover painting and illustrations by Willem G. Van de Hulst, Jr.
Original translations done by Harry der Nederlanden and Theodore Plantinga
for Paideia Press, St. Catharines-Ontario-Canada.
The publisher expresses his appreciation to John Hultink of Paideia Press for
his generous permission to use his translation (ISBN 0-88815-503-4).

Edited by Paulina Janssen

ISBN 978-1-928136-03-3

All rights reserved © 2014, by Inheritance Publications
Box 154, Neerlandia, Alberta Canada T0G 1R0
Tel. (780) 674 3949
Web site: www.inhpubl.net
E-Mail inhpubl@telusplanet.net

Published simultaneously in U.S.A. by Inheritance Publications
Box 366, Pella, Iowa 50219

Printed in Canada

Contents

1. By the Window

Bruno was sitting on the window sill — by the window.
Bruno was a bear.
Bruno was a chubby, cuddly teddy bear.

He was always laughing. He always laughed with his one eye. Do you know why?

One of his eyes was black; but the other one was a glass button. It twinkled and twinkled. The sun shone.

It shone right on Bruno's glass eye.

Look, the goof! He winked.

It was just as if he had a secret joke!

Rosie was sitting in a
big chair — also by the
window.
Rosie was a girl.
Rosie was a dear two
year old girl.

Oh, but what was the
matter with Rosie?
She did not laugh; she did not play. She just sat
quietly in the big chair. Her head hung to one side.
Look . . . !
Her cheeks were flushed; her hands were so warm.
And her brown eyes glistened so . . . so strangely.
Why was that?
Rosie was sick.
She had a fever.
Poor child! Her head ached and ached.

2. The Goof

There came Mother.
She knew that Rosie was not feeling well.
She had made Rosie's bed ready for her.
"Come, dear. Come with Mother. Rosie is going to

take a little nap. Tomorrow you will feel a lot better. Come with Mother, little sweetheart."

There went Rosie.
She sat on Mother's arms. Her head leaned on Mother's shoulder . . . Oh, her head was so tired — her head was so sore.
But Rosie still said something, very softly. "Bwuno too. Bwuno come to bed too."

"Oh, yes! Silly Mother! I forgot all about Bruno. Yes, dear. Bruno will come too. Bruno is not feeling well either, is he? Come along, Bruno. You can go under the blankets together — Rosie and Bruno. Two sweet children. Hold on to Bruno! Oh, his head is also sore . . ."

Mother walked toward the door.
She had wrapped Rosie in a blanket.
"Come, dear!"
But, look! What was that slipping out from under the blanket?

It was Bruno.

First came his legs, then his tummy, and then . . .

Oh, look! He came out all the way!

Rosie did not know. And Mother did not know either.

Rosie's little hand was so tired.

That little hand let Bruno go.

He slid down Mother's back; he slid down Mother's skirt.

Thump! There he sat, the little goof, his back against the doorpost.

His glass eye twinkled.

He winked.

It was just as if he had a secret joke!

3. An Idea

Clumpetty-clump! Clumpetty-clump!

Who was coming up the stairs?

Who was laughing so hard?

Who was making all that racket?

Oh, yes . . . ! Jimmy and Joe of course.

They were a pair of noisy rascals.

They had been playing outside on the street. But it was getting dark, time to go inside. They did not know that Rosie was sick.

They burst in.

Father was not home yet.

But where was Mother? Where was Rosie? There was no one! Where was everyone?

Oh, look! Bruno, the bear, he was home!

There he sat.

And he laughed at them with his one eye.

Jimmy grabbed him.

"Hi, Bruno. Can you somersault?"

That rowdy Jimmy threw the bear high into the air. And that wild Bruno dove with his head right into Mother's sewing basket.

But Jimmy grabbed him again.

Joe stood by the table.

Joe was the oldest. Joe was the biggest. Joe was the wildest.

Joe had found some string on the street, long and thin and in a tangle. He was untangling the knots. He mumbled to himself.

Jimmy thought, "I'm going to scare Joe."

Thump!

Bruno got a shove. Bruno jumped right onto Joe's string.

Joe mumbled more loudly. "Cut it out," he said but then he couldn't help but laugh.

Suddenly he had an idea.

He tied the end of the string around Bruno's neck. Now Bruno had to dance. "A-one and a-two and cha-cha-cha."

Jimmy and Joe danced along.

Poor Bruno. He was jerked around the room on the end of the string!

Those roughnecks!

If Mother saw them . . . !

If Father heard it . . . !

If sick little Rosie knew what was going on . . . !

Father brought Bruno home some time ago. Father had been fixing the chimney in a big, fancy house. He had seen Bruno lying in a corner of the attic.  The maid had said, "I'll toss that old thing out with the trash."

But Father had said, "Could I take it home with me

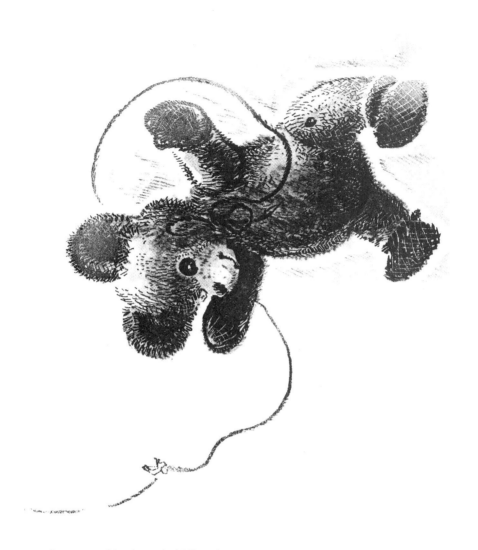

for my little girl?" That had been all right with the maid.

Bruno had looked very old and tattered. He only had one eye, half a nose, and no soles on his feet. But little Rosie thought he was beautiful, just beautiful. Mother had made him look a lot better.

She had sewed a glass button on his head. Now he had two eyes again. She had sewed up his poor nose with black wool. Now he had a round nose again. And she had sewed two patches of bright red wool on his tattered feet. Then, with his red socks on, he was a well-dressed teddy bear.

Mother was proud of the new Bruno. So was Father. But little Rosie loved Bruno most of all. She took him with her wherever she went.

But now look! Just look at those roughnecks!
If Mother saw them . . . !
If Father heard it . . . !
If sick little Rosie knew what was going on . . . !

4. What Fun

Look, look . . . !
Those naughty boys!
The window was standing open.
And Joe said, "Oh, Jimmy, I have an idea . . . yes . . . Should we?"
"Should we what?"
"Come!"

Oh, there he went, that poor Bruno. Just like that, there he went right out the window. Just a little ways.

Jimmy was scared. "Oh, look out!"

But Joe said, "Don't worry. This string is plenty strong."

There went Bruno — a little lower and then a little lower still.

And down below them was the water, the cold, deep water of the canal.

What fun! The two boys put their heads out of the window to watch Bruno. Bruno had to dance again. "Come on, Bruno! A-one and a-two and cha-cha-cha! Look at him go! Isn't he silly?"

His head was twisted to one side and his legs flopped this way and that . . .

The two boys shouted with laughter.

What fun! What a lot of fun this was!

A little lower . . . Just above the water.

But — what if Father would come by? Over there, on the other side of the canal?

No, Father was not coming.

An old woman did pass by. She shook her finger at the boys. "Watch out, you little rascals! Do you want that nice teddy bear to fall into the water?"

Jimmy and Joe just laughed at the old woman.

Of course not! Bruno wouldn't fall into the water. The string was plenty strong.

"Come on, Bruno! Come on, boy! Dance!

"Swing! Spin!

"Come on, Bruno! Come on, boy! Dance for us! A-one and a-two and cha-cha-cha!"

"Oh . . . oh . . . Joe! Joe! Mother is coming! Quick, quick!"

Jimmy pulled his head inside. He bumped it against the window. He did not even feel it. He got such a scare. He heard Mother's footsteps in the hall.

"Hurry, Joe. Hurry!"

Joe ducked inside too, trying to pull in the string. He pulled hard.

Hurry! Hurry!

Oh, but what was that? The string was stuck!
And Mother was right by the door.
Joe tugged . . . tugged.
Snap! went the string. It flew inside — but Bruno
was no longer on the end.
The string . . . had broken!

Jimmy dove under the table in fright. He looked around frantically, his heart pounding.
And Joe? Joe turned red as a beet. He, too, dove under the table. He, too, looked around frantically.
But there was nothing to be seen.
And the little piece of string trailed behind.
But Bruno — where was Bruno?
Oh, if Mother found out . . . !

5. Bruno on the Pole

Shhh . . . ! Mother was going back. Mother went to the kitchen.
Joe whispered, "Should we look? Do you dare?"
They flew to the window.
They stuck their heads outside.
They looked . . . they searched . . .
Where was Bruno? Where could he be? Had he drowned? Where was he?

Suddenly Jimmy cried out, "There he is! Over there! See? There he sits!"
Yes, there he sat — the goof.
His head was tilted to one side. His arms pointed straight out. There he sat — on a pole.

A short bit of pole stuck up out of the water close to the wall of the house.

It was very old and very black. A long, crooked nail stuck out of the top of the pole. Bruno was hooked on the nail.

He had not fallen into the water. He had not drowned after all. But Jimmy and Joe could not reach him. They could not even get close.

Maybe with a long stick? Or maybe with a long rope?

"Look out! Here comes Mother!"

Quickly the two boys pulled their heads inside again. Should they tell Mother? Should they say, "Mother, Bruno is sitting on a pole above the water — and it's our fault"?

But no, they were afraid; they didn't dare.

Mother would be so angry!

Mother came in.

She looked sad. She said, "Boys, your little sister is very sick."

Rosie sick? Jimmy and Joe stared at their mother with big eyes.

Rosie sick? They did not know that.

And they thought to themselves, "If only we hadn't played with her teddy bear! What if he falls off the pole and floats away? What if he sinks to the bottom of the canal? Poor Rosie! If only we had not done it . . . !"

They sneaked a quick look at the window

They both blushed with shame.

But Mother did not notice.

She said, "Joe, will you go and pick up some oranges for me? From the corner store? Rosie would like that. The poor dear is so thirsty! But hurry right back."

"Yes, Mother."

Joe gave Jimmy a nudge with his elbow.

Then Jimmy said, "May I go too, Mother?"

"You? All right. But hurry."

Oh, good! Now they could both go outside. They could both get a good look from the other side of the canal. Would Bruno still be there?

18

They walked down the hallway.

Shhh! Listen. Rosie was crying. Listen, she called, "Bwuno! Bwuno! Bwuno come."

The two boys were frightened.

They tiptoed down the stairs and out the door.

Outside the street lights were already on.

6. Bruno the King

The two boys ran down the street to the store on the corner.

Quickly they bought their oranges.

And then . . . ?

Did they hurry home . . .? Did they hurry back to Rosie?

No, not yet.

Look, they walked further on. And then they turned down the next street.

Then they came to a bridge.

They walked across the bridge.

Look — they were on the other side of the canal.

Slowly they walked along the far bank.

They looked and looked.

It was getting darker and darker. Was Bruno still there? Or . . . ?

They peered across the water.

Over there. That was their house. And there was the open window.

And under that window just above the water?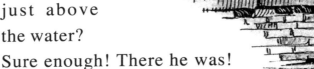

Sure enough! There he was! There he sat!

There he sat on the pole — like a king on his throne.

But the water was so wide.

Bruno was far out of reach.

The water glittered.

And Bruno's one eye glittered too.

He laughed, the little goof. But he was far, far out of reach.

Joe said, "If only I could swim . . ."

Jimmy said, "If only I could fly . . ."

"If only we had a rowboat . . ."

"Yes . . . or if a barge would come by . . . Then I would say, 'Sir, would you please grab that teddy bear over there and throw it to us?' Yes, that's what I would say."

But no barge came by. And they had no rowboat. And they could not swim.

It was very quiet and very lonely along the dark canal.

Jimmy found a big rock.

He threw it. "Splash!" went the rock.

Large ripples spread over the water. The ripples spread to the black pole and it shook a little. Bruno's head shook too, almost as if he were saying, "No! Don't! Don't!"

That scared Joe. He gave Jimmy a shove.

"Don't! What if Bruno falls off?"

Along the canal came a big dog.

Suddenly Joe said, "I know! Dogs are good swimmers."

Joe called to the dog. He pointed across the canal to Bruno. He urged the dog on, "Get him, boy! Get him!"

He thought the dog might dive right into the water. "Get him, boy! Get him!"

But oh, no! Those poor boys!

"Woof, woof!" barked the big dog.

He was a noisy, mean dog. He did not go for Bruno — he went for the two boys instead.

They had said, "Get him, boy! Get him!"
Just wait! He would get them — both of them.
"Woof, woof!"
His white teeth gleamed.

Oh, Jimmy was terrified. He ran off.
And Joe ran right behind him.
One of the oranges fell but he managed to grab it.
"Woof, woof! Woof, woof!"
The noisy dog ran right behind them.

And Bruno — the goof — sat on his pole . . . like a
king on his throne.

7. Bruno is Gone

It was night.

The house was quiet and very dark.

All the children were sleeping.

All the children? No, not all of them.

Just look in that little bed.

Just look at that little girl.

She was not sleeping. She could not sleep.

Her head ached. She was burning with fever.

She thrashed around in her bed, looking for something. But she could not find it.

She cried and called out, "Bwuno! Bwuno, come! Bwuno, bad boy. Bwuno, come to Rosie."

But Bruno did not come.

Mother came instead.

Mother came every time Rosie called.

She gave Rosie something to drink. She whispered soothing words to her. But Bruno? No, she did not know where Bruno was. Bruno was gone. What could have happened to him?

Mother had looked everywhere — everywhere. Where could that little bear be? She just could not understand it.

She was sad. If only she could help her girl and find Bruno for her . . . ! Then Rosie would go to sleep and forget about her pain.

"But dear, Mother cannot find Bruno. We'll find him tomorrow. Go to sleep now . . . Mother will look one more time."

But she could not find him anywhere.

And Rosie sobbed with grief.

Poor little Rosie!

And upstairs, in the attic? Jimmy and Joe lay in the big bed together.

But they were not asleep either.

Jimmy had been the first to wake up.

He heard Rosie call, "Bwuno! Bwuno, bad boy. Bwuno, come to Rosie."

Oh, Jimmy was frightened. He crawled deeper under
the blankets, but he still heard her voice. It sounded
so sad!

Jimmy woke Joe up.

Softly he whispered, "Listen, Joe! Rosie is crying."

Joe listened too. "Yes, that is Rosie. If only we
hadn't done it . . . ! It's our fault."

They both ducked down deep under the blankets.
But they listened closely.

They could still hear her sad voice calling.

It hurt them to hear that sound. They hurt deep
down inside, in their hearts.

Joe quietly folded his hands. He wanted to pray,
but somehow he did not dare.

When he had gone to bed, he had not prayed either.
He quickly dove under the blankets not daring to
pray.

Jimmy had said his prayer as he knelt next to his bed. He had said it as fast as he could. And that was not really praying. No, Jimmy did not really dare to pray either.

They had done something wrong. They knew that.

And they had not told Mother about it.

That was why they were afraid to pray.

God saw everything; He knew.

But they could still hear that voice. Listen.

Rosie sobbed, "Bwuno! Come, Bwuno."

But Bruno did not come.

8. Bruno in the Moonlight

It was night.

It was very dark and very quiet.

But the moon peeked from behind a cloud.

The moon saw something. Oh, it made him smile.

He saw the tall houses and the still water.

But there, rising out of the still water was a pole.

And on the pole sat a teddy bear, a cuddly, brown teddy bear. He was wearing red socks and his head was tilted to one side.

Splash!

What was that?

Ripples spread across the water.

What had happened?

It was a rat! A great big, black water rat.

It swam in the canal. It saw Bruno and thought, "What a funny looking animal!"

But the rat was not afraid of Bruno, not at all. He swam to the pole and climbed it. He sniffed and he snorted.

Snap! He bit Bruno's red sock.

Poor Bruno!

The bear wobbled back and forth, back and forth.

Oh, what if he fell?

The rat thought, "What an awful taste! Bah! I sure don't like that!"

Splash! He jumped back into the water. He ducked back into a dark hole in the wall.

He was gone! What a relief!

And then the night was silent once again.

Step . . . ! Step . . . ! Step . . . !
Someone was coming along the canal. He walked
very slowly, his hands behind his back. Step . . . !
Step . . . ! Step . . . !
Who was it?

It was a tall policeman.
There he came. Step by step.
Suddenly he stopped.
He saw something — something strange.
Over there, across the water. Over there, by the
houses, on a pole. There was something sitting on
the pole.
He leaned forward
over the water to get
a better look.
Then he laughed out
loud. "It's a teddy
bear wearing red
socks. Ha-ha-ha!"

The moon thought it
was funny too.
He slid from behind
the cloud out into the
open. He shone down

on the tall policeman's cap and made it look like silver.

Then he shone down on Bruno's glass eye, it twinkled merrily.

Bruno, that little goof, winked. He winked just as if he shared a secret joke with the policeman. He seemed to say, "Go on! Scoot! You can't catch me anyway."

The tall, friendly policeman laughed.
He looked at the houses and at their windows. He said to himself, "I wonder whose bear it is. Well, who knows? It probably belongs to one of those nice little children. Maybe it fell out of the window. Too bad! But I can't reach it. The canal is much too wide."
And then the tall policeman walked on again.
He walked very slowly, his hands behind his back.
Step . . . ! Step . . . ! Step . . . !

The wind sprang up and blew across the water.
It wanted to blow Bruno off his pole. Bruno wobbled. But the crooked nail held him fast.
The wind died down again.

Bruno wasn't afraid of anybody. He sat on his pole like a king on his throne.

The moon smiled once more and then he slipped away behind a cloud.

And then, once again, the night was very dark and very quiet.

9. Where Could He Be?

The next morning a light rain was falling.

Jimmy and Joe were walking to school.

They walked fast and they looked worried. Their voices were filled with sadness.

Jimmy said, "Where could he be?"

Joe wondered, "What could have happened to him?"

And they both said, "What if we never get him back . . . ?"

They walked to the end of the street. They turned down the next street. Across the bridge they went. Then they could look across the water.

Tears filled Jimmy's eyes.

Joe bit his lip. He was not going to cry because he was the oldest and the biggest. But it was terrible — just terrible.

What was the matter?

Early that morning Jimmy and Joe had quietly opened the window and looked down at the water . . . to the left . . . to the right . . .

Nothing!

Bruno was nowhere to be seen — nowhere at all.

How terrible!

Their little sister was still sick. She was burning with fever.

Joe had gone to take a quick look. He had peeked around the corner of her door.

Rosie was saying, "Bwuno, bad boy. Bwuno, not come."

Jimmy had gone to take a look too. Rosie said to him, "Jimmy get Bwuno? Jimmy get Bwuno for Rosie?"

Her voice sounded very small and sad.

The two boys had left quickly. They were sorry for what they had done. Very, very sorry. They loved their little sister very much. But what good did that do? It was all their fault that she was so sad.

They had not told anyone because they were afraid to tell.

No one knew — no one at all.

Now they were on their way to school. They walked along the canal.

They looked and looked across the water. Over there was their house. There was their window. And there, in the water, stood the black pole. Sticking out of the top of the pole was the large, crooked nail.

But . . . the pole was empty. They looked along the canal. They looked in all the dark corners. They looked up and down the canal.

But Bruno was nowhere to be seen, nowhere at all.

Could someone have grabbed him?

Could he have drowned?

How terrible! Bruno was gone!

Jimmy sniffed back his tears.

Quietly he said, "If only Mother knew what had happened!"

Joe answered him softly, "Shall we tell her? But I'm afraid to."

"I'm afraid to tell too," sniffed Jimmy.

They turned and started walking back.

"Do teddy bears cost a lot?" asked Jimmy.

"Oh, I'm sure!" said Joe. "A real one, a nice cuddly one? I'm sure they cost a lot! Far too much for us."

Father and Mother did not have much extra money. And Jimmy and Joe — they had no money at all. Buy a new teddy bear? They could never get that much money! Never ever!

They had to turn down the next street to go to school. They looked back once more at the water. And then once more. And then again.

But Bruno was gone. Gone forever.

Poor boys! They were very worried and so very sad. And they were very, very sorry for what they had done. But it was all their own fault.

10. Bruno the Football

A light rain was falling. Jimmy and Joe turned down the next street. They came to a playground lined with trees.

What a racket! What was going on?

A bunch of big, rough boys were playing football.
They were hollering and screaming and shouting
with laughter.
They were all running and kicking. But it was not a
real football.
Look, it flew high into the air.

Suddenly . . .
"Oh, Joe . . . Joe!"
Jimmy grabbed Joe by the arm.
"Joe! Oh, Joe! Look! That's not a football! Look!
It's . . . it's . . . !"

Look at Joe! What was he up to?
He dashed forward, right into the bunch of boys
playing football. Jimmy was right behind him.
Joe hollered, "Stop! Stop! That's our teddy bear!"
But those big, rough boys laughed at him, "Go
away! It's ours."
Joe yelled, "No, it isn't! It's ours! It's ours!"

Joe grabbed one of the big boys by the shirt and said, "Please give it back. It's ours! Honest! It's my sis . . ."

"Go away, little liar," growled the boy. "We got it from a boatman. I was there myself. Now go."

The boy pulled himself loose and shouted, "Come on! Let's play."

Joe was kicked on the leg and Jimmy was shoved hard. The big boys screamed and shouted with laughter. "Come on! Let's play!" And there went the football, high into the air.

But it was not a real football. It was a football with arms and legs; yes, it was poor Bruno!

He flew high between the branches of the trees. Then down he fell.

"Kick it! Kick it here!" the big, rough boys shouted at each other. One grabbed Bruno by the head. Another grabbed him by the leg.

That poor, poor Bruno . . . He cracked.

They pulled and they yelled and they shouted with laughter.

Joe's face turned red and he clenched his fists. It wasn't their teddy bear! It was his sick little sister's teddy bear. And they were going to kick it to pieces. Joe swallowed back his tears.

Madly he dashed into the bunch of boys. Howling with anger, he lashed and kicked in every direction. "You nasty bullies! Give me that, you bullies!" he screamed.

Surprised, the boys jumped back from the little madman. But then they shouted with laughter again. They weren't at all afraid of him.

One grabbed Joe by the collar.

Another clutched his leg.

They tugged him back and forth.

That poor, poor Joe . . . He screamed.

And Bruno?

Bruno fell to the ground between all those trampling feet. They trampled all over Bruno. They even stepped on his head.

But suddenly another little boy dove between all those trampling feet. They trampled right on his hands, but he did not care.

Look! Look! He got it!

He ran off, carrying the teddy bear.

Who was that little boy?

It was Jimmy!

11. That is Fair

Jimmy ran, ran.

He ran so fast that he almost tripped over his own feet. One shoe came off.

Quickly he snatched it up and pulled off the other shoe too.

Then he ran down the narrow street in his stocking feet. Under his arm was Bruno.

Oh, no! Watch out!

A big, strong boy saw Jimmy run off with Bruno.

"Stop him! Stop him! Stop that thief!" he shouted.

And he dashed after Jimmy.

With his long legs, he could run much faster.

He was catching up to Jimmy.

Look out!

Jimmy ran and ran until he was almost out of breath.

Suddenly . . . Thump!

He tripped and fell.

The big, strong boy was on top of him.

"Now I've got you, you little thief!"

"No, no!" screamed Jimmy. "You can't have him. No! He's ours!"

The big strong boy grabbed the teddy bear. But Jimmy wouldn't let go.

Poor Bruno. He cracked.

Crack! Off came his head!

Poor Bruno!

"Are you going to let go?" shouted the boy.

"No, no!" cried Jimmy. "He's ours!"

Someone came around the corner. It was the tall policeman. He walked very slowly, his hands behind his back. He saw the two boys. Then he made a few big steps.

"There! I got you!"

He grabbed them both, Jimmy with one hand and the big strong boy with the other. In an angry voice he growled, "Stop, you two! No fighting!"

The big boy said, "Yes, yes, but he . . . he . . ."

And Jimmy cried, "No, no, sir! It was him! He . . . he . . ."

Scowling, the policeman asked, "What happened?"

The boy said, "We got this teddy bear from a boatman. His barge was passing through the canal. He tossed the teddy bear to us."

"But it's ours! It's Rosie's!" howled Jimmy.

The policeman demanded, "Let me see that teddy bear."

Suddenly the tall policeman laughed. "I know this teddy bear. The little goof! Ha-ha-ha!"

He asked Jimmy, "Where do you live?"

"Over there, sir. Over there. We made the teddy bear dance outside the window. And then he fell. And then he was sitting on a pole."

The policeman laughed again. "Oh, yes. I saw him there last night. He even winked at me. Just as if he was sharing a secret joke. What's your name?

"Jimmy. Jimmy, sir."

"Here, Jimmy, the teddy bear is yours. That is fair." The big boy smiled and said, "I'm sorry. I didn't know. Sure, he can have the teddy."

Then the big policeman walked on slowly, his hands behind his back.

Step . . . ! Step . . . ! Step . . . !

And Jimmy?

Jimmy ran straight for home. His socks were torn.

His knee bled. His hands were black with mud. But he did not think about that.

He ran straight for home, straight up the stairs. Mother was not there. Mother had to run an errand.

But Rosie was home. She was lying in bed, deep
under the blankets.

Quickly Jimmy stuffed the teddy bear down into
the bed, first the head and then the rest of him.
Then he ran off again, down the stairs and out into
the street.
He didn't dare show up late for school!

Oh, his cheeks glowed with joy.
His eyes sparkled.
He was so happy.
Bruno was back!
Oh, how glad he was.

12. Bruno in Bed

Mother hurried to check on her sick girl asleep in bed. She climbed the stairs and stopped at Rosie's room. She listened but she heard nothing.

Rosie wasn't crying anymore or calling out.

Was she asleep? Maybe the pain was going away.

Quietly she listened at the door.

No, she heard nothing.

She stepped inside on her tiptoes.

Sure enough, Rosie was sleeping. Oh, what joy!

But . . . what was that?

Rosie had a black nose. There was mud on her nose! How could that be?

And what was that under the blanket? Oh, no, it was something wet.

Mother took hold of the dirty thing carefully, with her thumb and her finger.

Very carefully she lifted the dirty thing out from under the blankets.

What ever could it be?

It was . . . It was Bruno's head! But only his head.

Mother felt under the blanket again.

There! The rest of him was there too.

But how could that be?

Mother stared wide-eyed.
She did not understand it at all
— not at all.
Who could have done it?
Who broke the teddy bear?
Who made him so wet and dirty?
Who stuffed him into bed with Rosie?
Who had been in the house while she was gone?
No, Mother did not understand it at all.

But — Rosie was sleeping peacefully.
That was good! The pain must be going away. Her
nose was black, but that wasn't so bad.
She must have given Bruno a kiss. Mother laughed
at the thought of it.
She said to herself, "Sleep well, my black-nosed
little girl. I'm happy Bruno's back again. Now you
can be happy."

Mother took Bruno with her.

She said, "Come on, Bruno. You need a quick bath. The sun is shining again, so soon you will be dry. Then I'll sew your head back on. And when Rosie wakes up, you can crawl into bed with her again. How happy she will be to have you back!"

But . . . who could have done it?
Mother shook her head.
"I don't know. I just don't know."

13. Everything is Well Again

It was night once again.

It was very dark and very quiet.

All the children were sleeping.

Yes, Rosie was sleeping too.

Just look . . . she was not crying or calling anymore.

She was sleeping peacefully because she was getting better.

And Bruno sat beside her on the pillow.

He was standing guard.

The boys were sleeping too.

In their sleep they held on to each other like faithful friends.

Everything was well again.

Mother now knew what had happened.

Father knew too.

Jimmy and Joe had told them everything.

Father and Mother were angry when they heard about it.

Father said, "What you did was wrong. That was bad enough. But not telling us about it — that was even worse. That's what made you feel so afraid. You deserved to feel afraid."

But Father and Mother were not angry anymore.

Jimmy had a bandage on his knee.

Joe had a bandage on his cheek. He had gotten hurt too, fighting with all those big boys.

But now everything was well again.

When Mother brought them to bed that evening, she said, "Jimmy and Joe, what must you do now?"

They knew very well.

As they said their evening prayers, they also prayed, "Dear Lord, forgive us for what we did. We're very sorry."

Now they slept peacefully.
For everything was well again.

The tall policeman walked along the canal.
He looked at the pole. No one was sitting on it.
Still, he couldn't help laughing.
Slowly, he walked on — his hands behind his back.
Step . . . ! Step . . . ! Step . . . !

The moon peeked around the corner of a cloud.
He looked down at the pole too.
But there was nothing on it.
He looked through a window. As he shone into
Rosie's bedroom, he caught Bruno's one eye.
"Aren't you sitting on that pole anymore? Are you
back in the house? What happened?"

But Bruno just winked,
as if to share a secret
joke.
The little goof!

Titles in this series:

1. The Little Wooden Shoe
2. Through the Thunderstorm
3. Bruno the Bear
4. The Basket
5. Lost in the Snow
6. Annie and the Goat
7. The Black Kitten
8. The Woods beyond the Wall
9. My Master and I
10. The Pig under the Pew
11. Three Little Hunters
12. The Search for Christmas
13. Footprints in the Snow
14. Little Tramp
15. Three Foolish Sisters
16. The Secret Hiding Place
17. The Secret in the Box
18. The Rockity Rowboat
19. Herbie, the Runaway Duck
20. Kittens, Kittens Everywhere
21. The Forbidden Path